Dear Parent:

Congratulations! Your child is taking the first steps on an exciting journey. The destination? Independent reading!

STEP INTO READING® will help your child get there. The program offers five steps to reading success. Each step includes fun stories and colorful art. There are also Step into Reading Sticker Books, Step into Reading Math Readers, Step into Reading Phonics Readers, Step into Reading Write-In Readers, and Step into Reading Phonics Boxed Sets—a complete literacy program with something to interest every child.

Learning to Read, Step by Step!

Ready to Read   Preschool–Kindergarten
• big type and easy words • rhyme and rhythm • picture clues
For children who know the alphabet and are eager to begin reading.

Reading with Help   Preschool–Grade 1
• basic vocabulary • short sentences • simple stories
For children who recognize familiar words and sound out new words with help.

Reading on Your Own   Grades 1–3
• engaging characters • easy-to-follow plots • popular topics
For children who are ready to read on their own.

Reading Paragraphs   Grades 2–3
• challenging vocabulary • short paragraphs • exciting stories
For newly independent readers who read simple sentences with confidence.

Ready for Chapters   Grades 2–4
• chapters • longer paragraphs • full-color art
For children who want to take the plunge into chapter books but still like colorful pictures.

STEP INTO READING® is designed to give every child a successful reading experience. The grade levels are only guides. Children can progress through the steps at their own speed, developing confidence in their reading, no matter what their grade.

Remember, a lifetime love of reading starts wi

D1364306

Thomas the Tank Engine & Friends™

CREATED BY BRITT ALLCROFT

Visit us on the Web!
StepIntoReading.com
randomhouse.com/kids
www.thomasandfriends.com

Educators and librarians, for a variety of teaching tools, visit us at randomhouse.com/teachers

ISBN: 978-0-307-93150-4 (trade) — ISBN: 978-0-375-97092-4 (lib. bdg.)

Printed in the United States of America   10 9 8 7 6 5 4

THOMAS & FRIENDS™

Secret of the Green Engine

Based on The Railway Series
by The Reverend W Awdry

Illustrated by Richard Courtney

Random House 🏠 New York

Thomas is going

to Blue Mountain Quarry.

Thomas is happy
to help
at the quarry.

Thomas sees
a green engine.
He does not know
the engine.

Thomas follows
the green engine.

It speeds up.

Thomas speeds up, too.

The bridge is broken.

"Look out!"

peeps Thomas.

Screech!

The green engine stops.

"Who are you?"
asks Thomas.
The green engine
is scared.

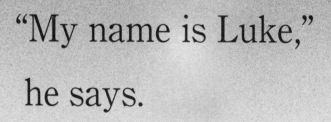

"My name is Luke,"
he says.
"I have to hide,
or I will be sent away."

Luke tells Thomas
that a long time ago,
he did a bad thing.

He bumped
a yellow engine,
and it fell into the water.
It was a mistake.

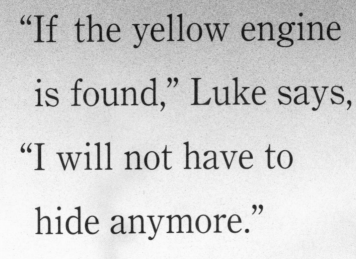

"If the yellow engine
is found," Luke says,
"I will not have to
hide anymore."

"I will find
the yellow engine,"
peeps Thomas.

Chug! Chug! Chug!
Thomas races
along the track.

Thomas searches

Tidmouth Sheds.

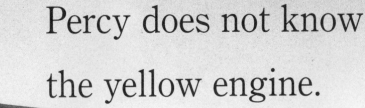

Percy does not know
the yellow engine.

Thomas chugs
to the docks.

Gordon does not know
the yellow engine.

Thomas visits
the Steamworks.
Victor knows
all the engines
on the Island of Sodor.

Thomas asks Victor
about the yellow engine.

"I was the yellow engine," says Victor.

Thomas is surprised.

Victor fell into the water.

Cranky saved him.

A fresh coat of paint
made Victor
clean and new.

Thomas has found
the yellow engine!
He races
to tell Luke.

Luke does not
have to hide.
Now he can
work at the quarry.

And now Thomas and
Victor have a new
friend!